The Tale Of Henrietta Hen

Arthur Scott Bailey

Copyright © 2023 Culturea Editions
Text and cover : © public domain
Edition : Culturea (Hérault, 34)
Contact : infos@culturea.fr
Print in Germany by Books on Demand
Design and layout : Derek Murphy
Layout : Reedsy (https://reedsy.com/)
ISBN : 9791041828692
Légal deposit : July 2023

THE TALE OF HENRIETTA HEN

I

A SPECKLED BEAUTY

Henrietta Hen thought highly of herself. Not only did she consider herself a "speckled beauty" (to use her own words) but she had an excellent opinion of her own ways, her own ideas — even of her own belongings. When she pulled a fat worm — or a grub — out of the ground she did it with an air of pride; and she was almost sure to say, "There! I'd like to see anybody else find a bigger one than that!"

Of course, it wouldn't really have pleased her at all to have one of her neighbors do better than she did. That was only her way of boasting that no one could beat her.

If any one happened to mention speckles Henrietta Hen was certain to speak of her own, claiming that they were the handsomest and most speckly to be found in Pleasant Valley. And if a person chanced to say anything about combs, Henrietta never failed to announce that hers was the reddest and most beautiful in the whole world.

Nobody could ever find out how she knew that. She had never been off the farm. But it was useless to remind her that she had never travelled. Such a remark only made her angry.

Having such a good opinion of herself, Henrietta Hen always had a great deal to talk about. She kept up a constant cluck from dawn till dusk. It made no difference to her whether she happened to be alone, or with friends. She talked just the same — though naturally she preferred to have others hear what she said, because she considered her remarks most important.

There were times when Henrietta Hen took pains that all her neighbors should hear her. She was never so proud as when she had a newly-laid egg to exhibit. Then an ordinary cluck was not loud enough to express her feelings. To announce such important news Henrietta Hen never failed to raise her voice in a high-pitched "Cut-cut-cut, ca-dah-cut!" This interesting speech she always repeated several times. For she wanted everybody to know that Henrietta Hen had laid another of her famous eggs.

After such an event she always went about asking people if they had heard the news — just as if they could have helped hearing her silly racket!

Now, it sometimes happened, when she was on such an errand, that Henrietta Hen met with snubs. Now and then her question — "Have you heard the news?" — brought some such sallies as these: "Polly Plymouth Rock has just laid an enormous egg! Have you seen it?" Or maybe, "Don't be disappointed, Henrietta! Somebody has to lay the littlest ones!"

Such jibes were certain to make Henrietta Hen lose her temper. And she would talk very fast (and, alas! very loud, too) about jealous neighbors and how unpleasant it was to live among folk that were so stingy of their praise that they couldn't say a good word for the finest eggs that ever were seen! On such occasions Henrietta Hen generally talked in a lofty way about moving to the village to live.

"They think enough of my eggs down there," she would boast. "Boiled, fried, poached, scrambled, or for an omelette — my eggs can't be beaten."

"If the villagers can't beat your eggs they certainly can't use them for omelettes," Polly Plymouth Rock told Henrietta one day. "Everybody knows you have to beat eggs to make an omelette."

Henrietta Hen didn't know what to say to that. It was almost the only time she was ever known to be silent.

II

A FINE FAMILY

Henrietta Hen's neighbors paid little attention to her boasting, because they had to listen to it so often. At last, however, there came a day when she set up such a cackling as they had never heard from her before. She kept calling out at the top of her lungs, "Come-come-come! See-what-I've-got! Come-come-come! See-what-I've-got!" And she acted even more important than ever, until her friends began to say to one another, "What can Henrietta be so proud about? If it's only another egg, she's making a terrible fuss about it."

They decided at last that if they were to have any peace they'd better go and look at whatever it was that Henrietta Hen was squawking about. So they went—in a body—to the place where she had her nest, in the haymow.

When Henrietta caught sight of her visitors she set up a greater clamor than ever.

"Well, well!" cried the oldest of the party, a rather sharp-tongued dame with white feathers. "What's all this hubbub about?" And then they learned what it was that Henrietta wanted them to see.

"Did you ever set eyes on such a fine family?" she demanded as she stepped aside from her nest and let them peer into it.

"A brood of chicks—eh?" said the lady in white. "Well, what's all the noise about?"

Henrietta Hen turned her back on her questioner.

"I knew you'd all want to have a look at these prize youngsters," she said to the rest of the company. "You'll agree with me, of course, that there were never any other chicks as handsome as these."

Henrietta's neighbors all crowded up to gaze upon the soft balls of down.

"This is the first family you've hatched, isn't it?" Polly Plymouth Rock inquired.

Henrietta Hen said that it was her first brood.

Her neighbors wanted to be pleasant. So they told her that her children were as fine youngsters as anybody could ask for. And the old white dame, squinting at the nestlings, said to Henrietta:

"They're the finest you've ever had.... But there's one of them that has a queer look."

All the other visitors tried to hush her up. They didn't want to hurt Henrietta Hen's feelings. It was her first brood of chicks; and they could forgive her for thinking them the best in the whole world. So when they saw that old Whitey intended to be disagreeable they began to cluck their approval of the youngsters, hoping that Henrietta wouldn't notice what Whitey said.

Nor did she. Henrietta Hen was altogether too pleased with herself and her new family to pay much attention to anybody else's remarks.

"I hope," said Henrietta, "that you'll all come to see my family often. As the youngsters grow, I'm sure they'll get handsomer every day."

The neighbors thanked her. And crowding about old Whitey they moved away. Old Whitey just had to go too. She couldn't help spluttering a little.

"What a vain, empty-headed creature Henrietta Hen is!" she exclaimed. "She doesn't know that one of her brood is nothing but a duckling!"

III

WET FEET

Somehow Henrietta Hen never noticed that one of her brood was different from the rest. They were her first youngsters and they all looked beautiful to her.

Just as soon as Henrietta began to take her children for strolls about the farmyard she taught them a number of things. She showed them how to scratch in the dirt for food, how to drink by raising their heads and letting the water trickle down their throats. She bade them beware of hawks—and of Miss Kitty Cat, too. And she was always warning them to keep their feet dry.

"Water's good for nothing except to drink," Henrietta informed her chicks. "Some strange people, like old dog Spot, jump right into it. And how they manage to keep well is more than I can understand. Dust baths are the only safe ones."

So much did she fear water that Henrietta Hen wouldn't even let her children walk in the grass until the sun had dried the morning's dew. And the first sprinkle of rain was enough to send her scurrying for cover, calling frantically for her chicks to hurry.

Now, there was one of her family that always lagged behind when the raindrops began to fall. And often Henrietta had fairly to drive him away from a puddle of water. She sometimes remarked with a sigh that he gave her more trouble than all the rest of her children together.

This was the youngster that Mrs. Hen's neighbors told one another was different from his brothers and sisters. But poor Henrietta Hen only knew that he was unusually hard to manage.

As her family grew bigger, Henrietta Hen took them on longer strolls, always casting a careful eye aloft now and then, lest some hawk should swoop down upon her darlings. And though no hawk tried to surprise her, something happened one day that gave Henrietta almost as great a fright as any cruel hawk could have caused her.

7

They had strayed down by the duck-pond—had Henrietta and her children, stopping here and there to scratch for some tidbit, or to flutter in an inviting dust-heap. Once they had reached the bank of the pond Henrietta began to wish she hadn't brought her family in thatdirection. For one of the youngsters—the one that never would hurry in out of the rain—insisted on toddling down to the water's edge.

"Come away this instant!" Henrietta shrieked, as soon as she noticed where he was. "You'll get your feet wet the first thing you know."

She never said anything truer than that. The words were scarcely out of her bill when the odd member of her family flung himself into the water. Or to be more exact, he flung himself upon it; for he floated on the surface as easily as a chip and began to paddle about as if he had swum all his life.

"Come back! Come back!" Henrietta Hen shrieked. "You'll be drowned—and you'll get your feet wet!"

IV

A SWIMMER

Henrietta Hen ran as fast as she could down the bank and stood as near the water as she dared, cackling loudly and flapping her wings.

Her child, who was swimming in the duck-pond, seemed to have no intention of minding her. Nor did he seem to have any intention of drowning; and as for getting his feet wet, he acted as if he liked that.

"What shall I do? Oh, what shall I do?" Henrietta Hen squawked. She made so much noise that some of her neighbors came a-running, to see what was the matter. And as soon as they discovered what had happened they began to laugh.

"We may as well tell you," they said to Henrietta Hen, "that that chap out there is a duckling. The water won't hurt him."

Henrietta Hen gasped and gaped. She was astonished. But she soon pulled herself together. And it was just like her to begin to boast.

"See!" she cried to her friends, and waved a wing toward the water with an air of pride. "There isn't one of you that has a child that can beat him swimming."

"I should hope not!" said Polly Plymouth Rock with a shrug of her fine shoulders. And all the others agreed that they wanted no swimmers in their families.

Henrietta Hen announced that she was sorry for them. "Every brood," she declared, "should have at least one swimmer in it." She began to strut up and down the edge of the duck-pond, clucking in a most overbearing fashion. Really, she had never felt quite so important before—not even when her first brood pecked their way out of their shells.

"There's nothing quite like swimming," Henrietta Hen remarked with a silly smirk. "If it weren't for getting my feet wet I'd be tempted to learn myself. No doubt my son could teach me."

"Your son!" the old white hen sniffed. "He's not your son, Henrietta Hen. Somebody played a joke on you. Somebody put a duck's egg under you while you were hatching your eggs. And I think I can guess who it was that did it."

For just a moment Henrietta Hen stood still. The news almost took her breath away. Her comb trembled on the top of her head. She even stopped clucking. And she looked from one to another of her companions as if in hopes of finding one face, at least, that looked doubtful.... Alas! Everybody appeared to agree with old Whitey.

"If this is so," Henrietta muttered at last, "it's strange nobody ever noticed before that there was a duckling in my brood."

"We knew from the very first!" Polly Plymouth Rock told her. "You were the only one on the farm that didn't see that one of your family was different from the rest."

All this time the young duckling was swimming further and further away. He seemed to have forgotten all about his foster mother.

Henrietta Hen took one long last look at him. She guessed that she might have stood there forever cackling for him to come back and he wouldn't have paid the slightest heed to her.

Then she gathered her children—her really own—about her. "Come!" she said to them, "We'll go back home now."

"What about him?" they demanded, pointing to the truant duckling who was bobbing about on the rippling water. "Aren't you going to make him come, too?"

"No!" said their mother. "We're well rid of him. He has been more trouble to me than all the rest of you.... To tell the truth, I never liked him very well."

V

CAUGHT BY MR. CROW

It wasn't far to the edge of the cornfield from the farmyard fence. And Henrietta Hen was quick to discover that the freshly ploughed and harrowed field offered a fine place to scratch for all kinds of worms and bugs and grubs.

Not being what you might call a wise bird—like old Mr. Crow—Henrietta didn't know that Farmer Green had carefully planted corn in that field, in long rows. She did exclaim, however, that she was in great luck when now and then she unearthed a few kernels of corn. But she wasn't looking for corn. She merely ate it when she happened to find any.

It is no wonder, then, that she was amazed when a hoarse voice suddenly cried right in her ear, almost, "You're a thief and you can't deny it!"

She jumped. How could she have helped it? And the voice exclaimed, "There! You're guilty or you'd never have jumped like that."

Turning, Henrietta saw that a black, beady-eyed gentleman was staring at her sternly.

"It takes Mr. Crow to catch 'em," he croaked. "He can tell a corn-thief half a mile away."

All this time Henrietta Hen hadn't said a word. At first she was too surprised. And afterward she was too angry.

"Why don't you speak?" he demanded. He dearly loved a quarrel. And somehow it wasn't much fun quarrelling with anybody when the other party wouldn't say a word.

Still Henrietta Hen didn't open her mouth. She puzzled Mr. Crow. He even forgot his rage (for it always made him angry if anybody but himself scratched up any corn).

"What's the matter with you?" he asked. "What's the reason you don't speak?"

"I'm too proud to talk with you," said Henrietta Hen. "I don't care to be seen speaking to you, sir."

"Ha!" Mr. Crow exploded. "Don't you think I'm as good as you are?"

"No!" said Henrietta Hen. "No, I don't!"

Mr. Crow was all for arguing with her. He began to tell Henrietta many things about himself, how he had spent dozens of summers in Pleasant Valley, what a great traveller he was, how far he could fly in a day. There was no end to his boasting.

Yet Henrietta Hen never looked the least bit interested. Indeed, she began scratching for worms while he was talking. And that made the old fellow angrier than ever.

"Don't you dare eat another kernel of corn!" he thundered. "If you do, I'll have to tell Farmer Green."

"He feeds me corn every day — cracked corn!" said Henrietta.

"Well, I never!" cried Mr. Crow. "What's he thinking of, wasting good corn like that?"

"Really, I mustn't be seen talking with you," Henrietta Hen told Mr. Crow. "If you want to know the answer to your question, come over to the barnyard and ask the Rooster. He'll give you an answer that you won't like."

And then she walked away with stately steps.

Mr. Crow watched her with a baleful gleam in his eyes. He knew well enough what Henrietta meant. The Rooster would rather fight him than not. And though Mr. Crow loved a quarrel, he never cared to indulge in anything more dangerous than harsh words.

"I don't know what the farm's coming to," he croaked. "Here's Farmer Green wasting corn on such as her — and cracking it for her, too!"

So saying, the old gentleman turned his back on Henrietta Hen, who was already fluttering through the farmyard fence. And thereupon he scratched up enough corn for a hearty meal, grumbling meanwhile because it wasn't cracked for him.

"Somehow," he muttered, "I can't help wishing I was a speckled hen."

VI

HENRIETTA COMPLAINS

There was another member of Farmer Green's flock, besides Henrietta Hen, that was proud. Nobody needed to look twice at the Rooster to tell that he had an excellent opinion of himself. He had a way of walking about the farmyard that said quite plainly that he believed himself to be a person of great importance. And it was true that things went according to his ideas, among the flock.

He was always spoken of as "the Rooster." For although there were other roosters in the flock, they were both younger and smaller than he, and he would never permit anybody to call them—in his hearing—anything but cockerels.

These cockerels usually took great pains to keep out of the Rooster's way. If they were careless, and he caught them napping, he was more than likely to make matters unpleasant for them. He knew how to make their feathers fly.

Now, Henrietta Hen thought that the Rooster behaved in a most silly fashion. She said it pained her to see him prancing about, with his two long, arched tail-feathers nodding as he walked. The truth was, Henrietta could not endure it to have any one more elegantly dressed than she. And there was no denying that the Rooster's finery outshone everybody else's. Why, he wore a comb on his head that was even bigger than Henrietta's! And he had spurs, too, for his legs.

But what Henrietta Hen disliked most about the Rooster was the way he crowed each morning. It wasn't so much the kind of crowing that he indulged in; it was rather the early hour he chose for it that annoyed Henrietta. He always began his Cockle-doodle-doo while it was yet dark. Then everybody in the henhouse had to wake up, whether he wanted to or not. And Henrietta Hen did wish the Rooster would keep still at least till daylight came. She often remarked that it was perfectly ridiculous for any one from a fine family—as she was—to get up at such an unearthly hour.

She said it was a wonder she kept her good looks, just on account of the Rooster's crowing.

"Why don't you ask him to wait until it's light, before he begins to crow?" Polly Plymouth Rock asked Henrietta one day.

"I'll do it!" cried Henrietta. Right then she called to one of the cockerels, who was near-by. "Just skip across the yard and ask the Rooster—" she began.

The cockerel broke right in upon her message.

"Oh! I can't do that!" he exclaimed. "I've never gone up to the Rooster and spoken to him. If I did, he'd be sure to fight me."

"Just tell him that I sent you," said Henrietta. And she made the cockerel listen to her message. But he wouldn't be persuaded. He told Henrietta that the Rooster would be sure to jump at him the moment he opened his mouth. "Besides," he added, "it wouldn't do any good, anyhow. The Rooster can't wait until after daylight, before he begins to crow."

"He can't, eh?" Henrietta Hen spoke up somewhat sharply. "I'd like to know the reason why!" And fixing her gaze sternly upon the Rooster, she marched straight across the farmyard towards him, to find out.

VII

WARNING THE ROOSTER

"Good Afternoon!" Henrietta Hen greeted the Rooster. He had not seen her as she walked towards him. And when she spoke he hastily arranged his two long tail-feathers in what he considered a more becoming droop.

"Good afternoon, madam!" he answered — for the Rooster prided himself that he was always polite to the ladies. "Er — there's nothing wrong, I hope," he added quickly as he noticed an odd gleam in Henrietta Hen's eye.

"Yes — there is," she said. The cockerels might fear the Rooster, but Henrietta certainly didn't. She considered him a good deal of a braggart. Indeed, she even had an idea that she could have whipped him herself, had she cared to be so unladylike as to fight. "I've been bothered for a long time because you crow so early in the morning. You make such a racket that you wake me up every day."

The Booster hemmed and hawed. Somehow he felt uncomfortable.

"That's unfortunate," he stammered. And then he had a happy thought. "Anyhow," he continued, with a smile at Henrietta, "you don't look as if you lacked for sleep, madam. You grow more beautiful every day."

Henrietta Hen admitted that it was so. "But," she said, "I believe I'd be even handsomer if I weren't disturbed so early. I don't like to get up while it's dark. So I'm going to ask you to delay your crowing, from now on, until after sunrise."

"Impossible!" cried the Rooster. "I'm sorry to disoblige you, madam. But what you ask can't be done."

"That's just what the cockerel said!" Henrietta Hen exclaimed.

"The cockerel!" the Rooster echoed angrily. "Which one? Has one of those upstarts been talking about me? Point him out to me and I'll soon teach him a lesson."

Henrietta Hen said that she hadn't noticed which cockerel it was. Somehow they all looked alike to her.

"Good!" the Rooster cried. "Then I'll have to whip them all, to make sure of punishing the guilty one." He looked very fierce.

"Don't be absurd!" Henrietta told him. "I asked one of the cockerels to give you a message about not crowing so early. And he declined. He said it wouldn't do any good."

"It wouldn't have done him any good," the Rooster declared, stamping a foot and thrusting his bill far forward, to show Henrietta Hen how brave he was.

"What's the matter?" she inquired. "Have you eaten something that disagrees with you?"

The Rooster couldn't help looking foolish. Henrietta Hen believed in letting him know that she stood in no awe of him. And while he was feeling ill at ease she hastened to tell him that hereafter he must hold onto his first crow until after sunrise.

"I can't do that," he told her again, unhappily.

"Don't you dare let go of it!" she warned him. "If that first crow gets away from you while it's dark, there'll be so many others to follow it that I shan't be able to close an eye for even a cat-nap."

VIII

WHY THE ROOSTER CROWED

Henrietta Hen had commanded the Rooster to wait until daylight before he began to crow.

He saw that she had made up her mind that he must obey her. But he knew he couldn't. And he always took great pains to be polite to the ladies.

It was a wonder the Rooster didn't turn red in the face. He had never found himself in such a corner before.

"You don't understand," he blurted. "I'd be delighted to oblige you, but if I didn't crow until after the sun rose I'd never crow again."

"We could stand that," was Henrietta Hen's grim reply.

"Perhaps!" he admitted—for she made him feel strangely humble. "But could you stand it if the night lasted forever?"

"You're talking nonsense now," she declared.

"You don't understand," he told her again. "And I must say I'm surprised, madam, that you didn't know it was I that waked the sun up every morning. That's why I crow so early."

Henrietta Hen was so astonished that she didn't know what to say. She thought deeply for a time—or as deeply as she could.

"Have you not noticed," the Rooster inquired, "that the sun never rises until I've crowed loudly a good many times?"

"No! No—I haven't," Henrietta murmured. "But now that you speak of it, I see that it's so."

"Exactly!" he said. "And often, madam, I have to crow a long time before he peeps over Blue Mountain. It's lucky I have a good, strong voice," the Rooster, added with a smirk, for he was feeling more at his ease. "If I had a thin, squeaky crow such as those worthless cockerels have, Farmer Green would have had to do many a day's work in the dark."

18

"Goodness!" Henrietta Hen gasped. "Do crow your loudest the moment you wake up, Mr. Rooster! Do make all the noise you can!" And he promised faithfully that he would.

Henrietta left him then. Somehow she couldn't get their talk out of her mind. And soon she had an unhappy thought. What if anything should happen to the Rooster's voice?

The moment that question popped into her head, Henrietta Hen hurried back to the Rooster.

"Do be careful!" she besought him. "Don't get your feet wet! For if you caught cold you might be so hoarse that you couldn't speak above a whisper."

The Rooster thanked her politely for thinking of his health.

"I always take good care of myself," he assured her.

"It looks like rain this minute," she said as she cast an anxious glance at the sky. "Hadn't you better run into the barn?"

He thought otherwise—and said as much.

"You ought to wear rubbers every day," she chided him, as she went away again.

Soon Henrietta returned once more to urge the Rooster to carry an umbrella. And it wasn't long after that when she came bustling up to him and informed him that a warm muffler about his throat wouldn't be amiss.

There seemed to be no end to her suggestions. And though at first the Rooster had liked to hear them (without having any idea of following them) after a time Henrietta's attentions began to annoy him.

"Great cracked corn!" he exclaimed. "This Henrietta Hen is getting to be a pest."

IX

HAUGHTY HENRIETTA

Feeling as important as she did, Henrietta Hen liked to have her own way. She said that she couldn't be expected to do just as others wished.

"I'll take orders from nobody," she often declared. "And if I lay eggs for Farmer Green I shall lay them when and where I please."

Henrietta took special delight in laying her eggs in out-of-the-way places. She was never content to lay two in the same nest.

"If they left them for me perhaps I'd feel differently," she explained to her neighbors. "But Johnnie Green gathers every egg that he can find. And if he takes my eggs I'll make him hunt for them, anyhow."

The older, more staid hens shook their heads when Henrietta talked like that. They told her she was ungrateful.

"Farmer Green gives you a snug home and plenty of food," they reminded her. "And the least you can do is to repay him. You ought not to make trouble by hiding your eggs."

But Henrietta Hen couldn't—or wouldn't—agree with them.

"It's all very well for you to talk," she retorted. "If my eggs were undersized I shouldn't mind losing them as fast as I laid them. But I lay the biggest and finest eggs to be had. So it's only natural that I should like to have at least one around to look at—and to show to callers."

Now, there were plenty of other hens in the flock that laid eggs exactly as big—or even bigger—than Henrietta Hen's. Some of them told her as much. Yet it did them no good to talk to her. She wouldn't believe that there were any eggs in the world to compare with hers. So her neighbors learned after a while that they might as well let Henrietta Hen manage her affairs as she pleased. They couldn't help hoping, however, that somehow Farmer Green would find a way to outwit her.

"What can Henrietta Hen be so boastful about now?" the hens asked one another one day. "She acts as if she thought more highly of herself than ever."

They soon discovered the reason for Henrietta's unusually pompous manner. For she began to make calls on all her friends. And she invited everybody to come to her latest nest high up in the haymow.

"I've something there to show you," she said with an air of mystery. "You'll be surprised to see it."

Most of Henrietta's neighbors did not show any great curiosity to see the surprise. They smiled at one another. "She's laid another egg—that's all!" they whispered.

But there are always some that can't rest until they know everybody else's business. And it was lucky that Henrietta Hen hurried home to receive her callers, because she had a good many. They came even earlier in the afternoon than was strictly fashionable. And they came in a crowd, too. That, however, didn't bother Henrietta Hen. Nor could they have arrived too soon to suit her.

"Look!" she cried, when they reached her nest high up in the haymow. "Did you ever see anything to beat that"

X

THE BIG, WHITE EGG

When Henrietta Hen's callers crowded about her nest in the haymow they expected to see something wonderful. But when they craned their necks and peered into the little hollowed-out snuggery in the hay they couldn't help being disappointed. And when they didn't burst forth with cries of surprise and praise Henrietta Hen looked quite unhappy.

"I thought," she said, "you'd want to see this egg. I'm sure you never beheld a bigger nor a whiter one than this."

They admitted that the egg was big and that it was very, very white. And if their praise was faint, Henrietta never noticed it.

"Are you going to let Farmer Green have that egg?" one of the company inquired.

"No doubt Johnnie Green will grab it as soon as he finds my nest," said Henrietta with something like a sigh. "If I could only keep this one I wouldn't care how many others he took."

Polly Plymouth Rock turned to old Whitey, a hen who had come with her to the haymow.

"What do you think?" Polly asked. "Is Henrietta in danger of losing this egg that she thinks so much of?"

"She needn't be alarmed," old Whitey answered. "If Johnnie Green robs her of this one, I'll miss my guess."

"Oh! I'm glad to hear you say that!" Henrietta Hen cried. "Now I won't need to worry—that is, if you know what you're talking about."

That, of course, was a most impolite way for Henrietta Hen to speak to anybody of old Whitey's age. Whitey was the oldest hen in the flock. And what she didn't know about such things as nests and eggs and roosts wasn't worth knowing.

Polly Plymouth Rock didn't like Henrietta Hen's remark. She opened her mouth.

And no doubt she would have said something quite sharp in reply. But old Whitey stopped her.

"Never mind!" said Whitey. "The day will come when Henrietta Hen will agree that my guess is a good one."

Still Henrietta Hen felt uneasy about that big, white egg.

"I do hope Johnnie Green won't find this new nest of mine," she remarked.

"If he does, I fear he'll take my beautiful egg away from me."

"Lay another!" said old Whitey. "Lay another and he'll take that and leave this one."

"I suppose I may as well try your scheme," Henrietta replied, "since nobody suggests anything better."

"My idea's a good one, or I'll miss my guess," said old Whitey.

There was some snickering among Henrietta Hen's callers as they bade her good afternoon and left her.

"They're laughing at old Whitey," she said to herself. She hadn't the slightest notion that they could be giggling at her. "Old Whitey must be wrong," she thought. "But I may as well take her advice, for I don't know what else to do."

Not long afterward Henrietta Hen came fluttering down from the haymow, squawking at the top of her lungs for old Whitey. And as soon as she found her, Henrietta cried, "Come up to my nest right away! I want to ask your advice."

Although she didn't say "Please!" old Whitey went with her.

OLD WHITEY'S ADVICE

Old Whitey—the most ancient hen in the flock—scrambled with some difficulty up to the top of the haymow in Farmer Green's barn. She could scarcely keep up with Henrietta Hen, whom she was following—by request. And when she arrived, breathless, at Henrietta's nest that proud and elegant creature turned a troubled face toward her.

"See!" said Henrietta. "I've taken your advice and laid another egg. But it's nothing like the beautiful, big, white one. This last egg is much smaller; and it's brown."

Old Whitey nodded her head. "Well!" she said. "What's your difficulty?"

"Don't you think," said Henrietta, "that if Johnnie Green finds my nest he'll be sure to take both eggs?"

"No, I don't," was old Whitey's blunt answer.

"Then he'll be sure to take the big, white one," Henrietta Hen wailed.

"No, he won't," old Whitey told her. "If he does, I'll miss my guess."

Well, that was really too much for Henrietta Hen to believe.

"That boy will never take a little egg and leave a big one," she declared.

"You wait and see if he doesn't," old Whitey advised her.

So Henrietta waited. Though she had little faith in old Whitey's advice, Henrietta could think of nothing else to do. And the next morning, to her great surprise, when Johnnie Green climbed into the haymow and found her nest he took the small brown egg and put it in his hat. And he never touched the big, white egg at all. He didn't even pick it up and look at it!

Perched on a beam overhead Henrietta Hen watched him breathlessly. And as soon as he had gone she went flopping down to the barn floor and set up a great clamor for old Whitey.

"What is it now?" old Whitey asked, sticking her head inside the doorway.

"Your guess was a good one!" cried Henrietta Hen. "He came; and he took the small one."

"There!" said old Whtiey. "I told you so! I knew Johnnie Green wouldn't rob you of that big egg. And if you keep laying small eggs in that same nest you'll find he'll let you keep the big one."

Henrietta Hen fairly beamed at her companion.

"How delightful!" she exclaimed. "I've become very, very fond of that big egg. I love to look at it. But there's another thing that worries me now. If that big egg should get broken—"

"Don't let that trouble you!" said old Whitey.

"I'm almost afraid to sit on my nest," Henrietta Hen confessed. "If the shell of that egg should happen to be thin—"

Old Whitey seemed much amused by Henrietta's fears.

"Let me know if you break it," she said. And then she left Henrietta with her treasure.

"I'll be very careful," Henrietta called after the old dame.

XII

PLAYING TRICKS

Now, the hen known as old Whitey was something of a gossip. She went straight to the farmyard and told everybody what had happened—what Henrietta Hen had said to her and what she had said to Henrietta Hen. The whole flock had a great laugh over the affair.

To Henrietta Hen's delight, all her neighbors took a keen interest in the wonderful white egg. They asked her countless questions about it. Above all, they always took pains to inquire whether she had been so unlucky as to crack the shell. And if Henrietta hadn't displeased Polly Plymouth Rock one day, the truth might never have come out.

Anyhow, Polly Plymouth Rock told Henrietta Hen that if she had any sense she would stop making such a fuss over a china egg.

"China egg!" cried Henrietta. "I don't know what you mean."

"That's not a real egg that you're so proud of," Polly Plymouth Rock declared. "It's nothing but a make-believe one. Johnnie Green left it in your nest to fool you, so you'd keep that nest and lay eggs in it, right along.... You're so careful not to break that china egg! Why, if youtried to break it you'd find that it's solid as a rock."

Henrietta Hen couldn't believe the terrible news.

"I laid that egg myself!" she shrieked.

"You think you did; but you didn't," Polly Plymouth Rock snapped. "Johnnie Green took an egg of yours one day and left that other one in its place, to deceive you. And everybody on the farm—except you—knows that he succeeded."

Henrietta Hen didn't wait to hear anything more. She rushed squalling into the barn and went straight to her nest. One good, hard peck at the big white egg told her beyond all doubt that she had been betrayed. The beautiful, big, white egg wasn't an egg after all!

Now that Henrietta Hen knew it she wondered how it could ever have deceived her. She saw that it was shiny and altogether unlike any egg she had ever seen anywhere.

"Johnnie Green has played a mean trick on me," Henrietta Hen cackled. "And now I'll play one on him! He can have his old china egg. I'll leave it here for him. But he'll find none of my beautiful little brown eggs beside it. I'll have my nest where he'll never discover it—not if he hunts for it all summer long!"

So saying, she left the haymow. And going into the carriage shed, her roving eyes chanced to light on an old straw hat of Johnnie Green's that lay upside down upon a high shelf.

Henrietta Hen managed to flutter up beside it. And then with many a chuckle she laid a brown egg in the hat.

"There!" she cackled. "This is the safest place on the farm. Johnnie Green hasn't had this hat on his head since last summer."

XIII

TWO IN A GARDEN

Jimmy Rabbit was enjoying a few nibbles at one of Farmer Green's cabbages. He hadn't noticed that there was anybody but himself in the garden. So it startled him to hear a shrill voice cry, "Get out of our garden!"

Jimmy Rabbit jumped. But he didn't jump far, for he soon saw that it was only Henrietta Hen speaking to him.

"Why should I get out of our garden?" Jimmy Rabbit inquired mildly.

"I should have said, 'Farmer Green's garden,'" said Henrietta Hen.

"Thank you very much for the warning; but I don't think we need go away just yet—if old dog Spot isn't sniffing around," said Jimmy Rabbit. "I don't believe there's any danger."

"You don't understand," Henrietta Hen cried. "I ordered you out of the garden."

"You ordered me?" said Jimmy Rabbit, acting as if he were astonished.

"Yes!" Henrietta declared. "And I'd like to know when you're going to obey me."

"It's easy to answer that," Jimmy Rabbit replied. "I'm going away as soon as I've finished my luncheon." Nobody could have been pleasanter than he. Yet Henrietta Hen seemed determined to be disagreeable.

"I don't see your lunch basket," she remarked, looking all around.

"No!" he replied. "I forgot it. I meant to bring one with me and carry a cabbage-head home in it."

Henrietta Hen spoke as if she were very peevish.

"You've no right," she said, "to take one of the cabbages away with you."

"I'm not going to," Jimmy Rabbit explained.

"You were nibbling at one when I first noticed you," Henrietta Hen insisted.

28

"Was I?" he gasped. "Are you sure you're not mistaken? Are you sure you weren't pecking at a cabbage-leaf yourself?"

Now, the truth of the matter was that Henrietta had herself come to the garden to eat cabbage. Really she was no better than he was. But somehow Henrietta Hen never could believe that she was in the wrong.

"You're impertinent," she told Jimmy

Rabbit in her severest tone. "You know very well that Farmer Green raises these cabbages for home use only."

"Well," said Jimmy Rabbit, "I'll make myself at home here, then." And turning a cold shoulder on Henrietta Hen he began nibbling at a cabbage-leaf once more.

Henrietta felt quite helpless. Somehow nothing she could say to the intruder seemed to have the slightest effect on him. And he appeared to be enjoying his luncheon so thoroughly that it made Henrietta Hen very hungry just to see him eat. In spite of herself she couldn't resist joining him at luncheon.

"Ah!" he exclaimed between mouthfuls, "I see you're making yourself at home, too."

Henrietta Hen tried to look very dignified. She pecked at the cabbage in an absent-minded fashion, pretending that it was no treat to her. As a matter of fact, she had been trying to get a taste of cabbage for a long while. And this was the first time she had managed to crawl through the garden fence. "One has to eat something," she murmured.

Jimmy Rabbit smiled slyly. Henrietta Hen couldn't deceive him. He knew that she was as fond of cabbage as he was himself.

"Did you ever hear it said," he asked her suddenly, "that eating too much cabbage causes long ears?"

XIV

EARS—SHORT OR LONG

Henrietta Hen's heart began to thump. She dropped a bit of cabbage out of her bill, letting it fall as if it burned her. And usually she was very careful as to her table-manners. "Goodness!" she said to Jimmy Rabbit, who was busily munching cabbage in Farmer Green's garden. "You frighten me!"

He had just asked her this strange question: "Did you ever hear it said that eating too much cabbage causes long ears?" And Henrietta Hen didn't want long ears. She knew they would be sure to spoil her beauty.

Jimmy Rabbit had no time to say anything more to Henrietta Hen. Although he had not finished his luncheon he left the garden suddenly— and in great haste. For old dog Spot began barking just beyond the fence; and Jimmy Rabbit always wanted to get as far from that sound as he could.

When Spot scurried into the cabbage-patch a little later Henrietta Hen called to him.

"What is it?" he asked her impatiently. "I'm in a great hurry. I don't like to stop."

"This is a very important matter," said Henrietta Hen. "Do you like cabbage?" she demanded.

"Cabbage?" he repeated after her as a puzzled look came over his face.

"You needn't act so surprised," Henrietta told him coldly. "You didn't come running into the garden for nothing. And I have reason to believe that you intended to eat some of Farmer Green's cabbages."

"What's your reason?" old Spot inquired.

"You have long ears," said Henrietta.

"Nonsense!" cried Spot. "What a person eats doesn't make his ears either long or short."

"Are you sure of that?" Henrietta Hen wanted to know.

"I've never eaten cabbage in all my life," he declared.

Still she couldn't rid herself of her fears.

"Perhaps," she said, "if you had eaten it your ears would have grown twice as long as they are now."

He shook his head. "I don't think so," he muttered.

"There's only one way to find out," Henrietta announced. "Eat a lot of cabbage—all you can! And we'll soon see whether your ears are growing longer."

But old dog Spot refused flatly to do anything of the sort. He said that his ears suited him quite well, just as they were.

"What!" Henrietta cried. "Wouldn't you eat cabbage to oblige a lady?"

Old Spot said he was sorry; but he had no liking for cabbage.

"How can you tell if you've never tasted it?" she asked.

He made no answer to that question. Instead, he asked her one of his own.

"Would you like long ears?" he inquired.

"Certainly not!" she cried.

"How can you tell if you've never tried wearing any?" he demanded.

"Don't be stupid!" she snapped. "None of my family wears ears that can be seen. What a sight I'd be with long ears! Ears are very ugly things, and I only hope that I haven't eaten so much cabbage that mine will begin to grow.... Do you suppose they'd hang down like yours or stick up like Jimmy Rabbit's? He didn't say anything about that."

Old dog Spot let out a howl.

"Jimmy Rabbit!" he growled. "Was he talking with you just before I arrived?"

"Yes!" said Henrietta. "It was he that asked me if I had ever heard that eating cabbage made a person's ears grow."

"I might have known that it was that young Rabbit who put such a silly notion into your head," Spot grumbled. "If you hadn't stopped me I'd have stopped him by this time.... But it's too late now."

"You don't suppose he was joking, do you?" Henrietta inquired.

"Of course he was," said Spot—and none too pleasantly.

"Well," Henrietta mused, as she pecked at a cabbage-leaf, "I must say that I think the joke's on you."

HENRIETTA'S FRIGHT

When the old horse Ebenezer stood in his stall in the barn he was always glad to talk with anybody that came along.

Henrietta Hen sometimes strolled into the horse-barn to see if she could find a little grain that had spilled on the floor. So it came about that she and Ebenezer had many a chat together. Henrietta had no great opinion of horses. She thought that they had altogether more than their share of grain.

But she was willing to pass the time of day with Ebenezer, because he let her walk right into his stall and pick up tidbits that had dropped upon the floor beneath his manger.

It was on such an occasion, on a summer's day, that he said to her with a sigh, "Haying's going to begin to-morrow."

Henrietta Hen remarked that she wasn't at all interested in the news. "And I don't see why you should sigh," she added. "Goodness knows you'll eat your share of the hay — and probably more — before the winter's over."

"It's the work that I'm thinking of," Ebenezer explained. "They'll hitch me to the hayrake and Johnnie Green will drive me all day long in the hot hayfields. I always hate to hear the clatter of the mowing machine," he groaned. "It means that the hayrake will come out of the shed next."

Henrietta Hen caught her breath.

"The mowing machine!" she gasped. "Is Farmer Green going to use the mowing machine now?"

"Certainly!" said Ebenezer. "I hear he's going to harness the bays to it to-morrow morning."

"My! my!" Henrietta wailed. "Isn't there any way I can stop him from doing that?"

"I don't know of any," Ebenezer told her. "I've often felt just as you do about it. There's nobody that dreads hearing the mowing machine more than I do."

"You can't feel the way I do," Henrietta declared.

"On the contrary," the old horse insisted, "I don't see how it can matter to you in the least. You don't have to pull the mowing machine nor the hayrake. Besides, didn't you just tell me that my news about haying didn't interest you?"

"But it does!" Henrietta cried. "I was mistaken. It means everything to me. It's the worst news I ever heard in all my life."

Old Ebenezer looked down at her with mild astonishment on his long, honest face.

"Why is it bad news?" he inquired. "If you'll tell me, perhaps I can help you."

So Henrietta Hen explained her difficulty. Whatever it was, it amazed Ebenezer. And he had to admit that he could think of no way out of the trouble.

"It was very, very careless of you," he told Henrietta. Then suddenly he had a happy thought. "Cheer up!" he cried. "If Farmer Green sits on them, maybe they'll hatch."

"Hatch!" she groaned. "They'll break!"

And she ran out of the stall and hurried into the yard.

She was just in time to hear Farmer Green calling to his son Johnnie.

"Look here!" said he. "I started to oil the mowing machine so I could use it to-morrow; and just see what I found in the seat!"

Johnnie Green came a-running. And there in the seat of the mowing machine, nestling in the hay which had been put there for a cushion the summer before, three eggs greeted Johnnie's eyes.

"They must belong to the speckled hen," Johnnie decided. "I knew she'd stolen her nest again. I couldn't find it anywhere." He picked up the eggs and put them in his hat. "She's a sly one," he said.

That remark made Henrietta Hen somewhat angry. At the same time she was glad that Farmer Green had discovered the eggs before it was too late. She wouldn't have liked him to sit on them.

It always upset her to see her eggs broken.

XVI

THE ROOSTER UPSET

During the summer Henrietta Hen roamed about the farmyard as she pleased. To be sure, she always came a-running at feeding time. But except when there was something there to eat, she didn't go near the henhouse. She "stole her nest," to use Johnnie Green's words, now in one place and now in another. And at night she roosted on any handy place in the barn or the haymow, under the carriage-shed or even over the pigpens.

However, when the nights began to grow chilly Henrietta was glad enough to creep into the henhouse with her companions. She always retired early. And being a good sleeper, she slept usually until the Rooster began to crow towards dawn. Of course now and then some fidgetty hen fancied that she heard a fox prowling about and waked everybody else with her squalls.

Such interruptions upset Henrietta. After the flock had gone to sleep again Henrietta Hen was more than likely to dream that Fatty Coon was in the henhouse. And she would squawk right out and start another commotion.

Luckily such disturbances didn't happen every night. Often nothing occurred to break the silence of the henhouse. And Henrietta would dream only of pleasant things, such as cracked corn, or crisp cabbage-leaves, or bone meal. After dreams of that sort Henrietta couldn't always be sure, when the Rooster waked her with his crowing, that she hadn't already breakfasted. But she would peck at her breakfast, when feeding time came, and if it tasted good she would know then that the other food had been nothing but a dream.

One night, soon after she had gone back to roost in the henhouse, it seemed to Henrietta that she had scarcely fallen asleep when the Rooster crowed.

She awoke with a start.

"Goodness!" she exclaimed under her breath. "I must have slept soundly, for I haven't dreamed a single dream all night long." Then she noticed that none of the other hens had stirred. "Lazy bones!" Henrietta remarked to the Rooster. "You won't get 'em up in a hurry. They, don't hear you at all."

To her surprise she received no answer.

"He couldn't have heard me," she said to herself. So she repeated her speech in a louder tone. And still the Rooster made no reply. Henrietta couldn't understand it, he was always so polite to the ladies. Could it be that he was snubbing her?

Henrietta grew a bit angry as that thought popped into her head.

"What's the matter?" she snapped. "Have you lost your voice? It was loud enough to wake me up a few moments ago."

Receiving no response whatsoever, Henrietta completely lost her temper. "I'll see what's wrong with you!" she cackled. And throwing herself off her roost, though it was dark as a pocket in the henhouse, she flung herself upon the perch just opposite, where she knew the Rooster had slept.

It was no wonder that Henrietta Hen blundered in the dark. It was no wonder that she missed her way and stumbled squarely into the Rooster, knocking him headlong on the floor.

He set up a terrible clamor. And he made Henrietta Hen angrier than ever, for he cried out in a loud voice something that would have displeased anybody. "A skunk is after me!" he bawled.

XVII

A SIGN OF RAIN

There was a terrible hubbub in the henhouse. The Rooster squalled so loudly that he waked up every hen in the place. And when they heard him crying that a skunk had knocked him off his roost they were as frightened as he was, and set up a wild cackle. All but Henrietta Hen! She knew there was no skunk there.

"Don't be a goose—er—don't be a gander!" she hissed to the Rooster. "I'm the one that bumped into you."

The Rooster quickly came to his senses.

"Don't be alarmed, ladies!" he called to the flock. "There's no danger. There's been a slight mistake." He pretended that he hadn't been scared. But he had been. And now he was somewhat uneasy about Henrietta Hen. He feared he was in for a scolding from her.

"If you had answered me when I spoke to you I wouldn't have left my perch in the dark," she told the Rooster severely. "When I moved to your perch to see what was the matter I blundered into you. And then you thought I was a skunk! You owe me an apology, sir!"

The Rooster was glad it was not lighter in the henhouse, for he felt himself flushing hotly.

"You must pardon me," he said. "I had no idea it was you, for you waked me out of a sound sleep."

"Sound sleep, indeed!" Henrietta Hen exclaimed with a sniff. "Why, you had been crowing only a few moments before. In fact it was your crowing that roused me."

"No doubt!" said the Rooster. "But you see, I fell asleep again immediately."

"Then you must be ill," Henrietta retorted, "for I've never known you to go to sleep again, once you've begun your morning's crowing."

"But it's not morning now," the Rooster informed her. "It's not even late at night—certainly not an hour since sunset."

Henrietta Hen was astonished.

"I noticed that the night seemed short," she muttered.

The Rooster thought it a great joke.

"Ha! ha!" he laughed. And he said to the rest of the flock, with a chuckle, "Henrietta thought it was morning! No doubt she'd have gone out into the yard if the door hadn't been shut." And the other hens all tittered. They always did, if the rooster expected them to.

Well, if there was one thing that Henrietta Hen couldn't endure, it was to be laughed at.

"Don't be silly!" she cried. "Why shouldn't I think it was morning, when he crowed almost in my ear?"

"Don't you know why I crowed?" the Rooster asked her. And without waiting for any reply, he said, "I crowed to let Farmer Green know it was going to rain to-morrow."

Of course Henrietta Hen had to have the last word. The Rooster might have known she would.

"Then," she observed, "I suppose you squawked to let him know there was a skunk in the henhouse."

XVIII

IN NEED OF ADVICE

Something was troubling Henrietta Hen. She seemed to have some secret sorrow. No longer did she move with her well-known queenly manner among her neighbors in the farmyard. Instead, she spent a good deal of her time moping. And no one could guess the reason. She didn't even care to talk to anybody—not even to boast about her fine, speckled coat. And that certainly was not in the least like Henrietta Hen.

Always, before, Henrietta had seized every chance to parade before the public. Now she seemed to crave privacy.

What was the matter? To tell the truth, Henrietta Hen herself did not know the answer to that question. That is to say, she did not knowwhy a certain thing was so. She only knew that a great misfortune had befallen her. And she dreaded to tell anybody about it.

To be sure, there was old Whitey—a hen who had lived on the farm longer than any other. Most members of the flock often asked her advice. Even Henrietta herself had done that. But this difficulty was something she didn't want to mention to a neighbor. If there were only somebody outside the flock to whom she could go for help! But she knew of no one.

Then Henrietta happened to hear of Aunt Polly Woodchuck. The Muley Cow, who went to the pasture every day, mentioned Aunt Polly's name to Henrietta. According to the Muley Cow, Aunt Polly Woodchuck was an herb doctor—and a good one, too. No matter what might be troubling a person, Aunt Polly was sure to have something right in her basket to cure it.

"I'd like to see her," Henrietta Hen had said. "But I can't go way up in the pasture, under the hill."

"Could you go to the end of the lane?" the Muley Cow inquired.

"Yes!"

"Then I'll ask Aunt Polly Woodchuck to meet you by the bars to-morrow morning," the Muley Cow promised.

That suited Henrietta Hen.

"I'll be there — if it doesn't rain," she agreed.

Early the next day she followed the cows through the lane. And she hadn't waited long at the bars when Aunt Polly Woodchuck came hobbling up to her. Being a very old lady, Aunt Polly was somewhat lame. But she was spry, for all that. And her eyes were as bright as buttons.

Henrietta Hen saw at once that Aunt Polly was hopelessly old-fashioned. She carried a basket on her arm, and a stick in her hand.

"Well, well, dearie! Here you are!" cried Aunt Polly Woodchuck. "The Muley Cow tells me you're feeling poorly. Do tell me all about yourself!]No doubt I've something in my basket that will do you a world of good."

XIX

AUNT POLLY HELPS

Somehow Henrietta Hen couldn't help liking Aunt Polly Woodchuck, in spite of her old-fashioned appearance. She certainly had a way with her—a way that made a person want to tell her his troubles.

"I don't know whether you can help me or not," said Henrietta Hen. "Have you any feathers in your basket?"

"No—no! No feathers!" Aunt Polly replied. "I use herbs in my business of doctoring. But I've heard that a burnt feather held under a body's nose will do wonders sometimes.... I must always carry a feather in my basket, hereafter."

"One feather wouldn't do me any good," said Henrietta Hen with a doleful sigh. "I need a great many more than one."

"You do?" Aunt Polly cried.

"Yes!" Henrietta answered. "Half my feathers have dropped off me. And that's why I've come to ask your advice. I'm fast losing my fatal beauty."

Henrietta Hen's voice trembled as she told Aunt Polly Woodchuck the dreadful news. "I don't believe you'll be able to help me," she quavered. "I'll soon look like a perfect fright. Besides, winter's coming; and how I'll ever keep warm with no feathers is more than I know."

Henrietta Hen couldn't understand how Aunt Polly managed to stay so calm. Henrietta had expected her to throw up her hands and say something like "Sakes alive!" or "Mercy on us!" But the old lady did nothing of the sort.

She set her basket down on the ground; and pushing her spectacles forward to the end of her nose, she leaned over and looked closely at Henrietta Hen. Aunt Polly's gaze travelled over Henrietta from head to foot and then back again. And she took hold of one of Henrietta's feathers and gave it a gentle twitch.

"Look out!" Henrietta cried. "You'll pull it out if you're not careful. And I can't afford to lose any more feathers than I have to."

"Don't worry!" Aunt Polly Woodchuck advised her. "Cheer up! There's nothing the matter with you. You are molting. You are going to get a new outfit of feathers for winter. Your old ones have to fall out in order to make room for the new. And no doubt the fresh ones will be much handsomer than the old."

Henrietta couldn't believe that Aunt Polly knew what she was talking about.

"I can't be molting as early in the fall as this," she protested. "I've never got my winter feathers so soon.... I fear you're mistaken," she told Aunt Polly.

"Oh, no! I'm not mistaken," Aunt Polly Woodchuck insisted. "I know it's early for molting—but haven't you noticed that the wheat grew big this year, and that the bark on young trees is thick? And haven't you observed that Frisky Squirrel is laying up a great store of nuts in his hollow tree, and that the hornets built their paper houses far from the ground this summer?"

Henrietta Hen's mouth fell open as she stared at Aunt Polly Woodchuck. And when the old lady paused, Henrietta looked quite bewildered.

"I don't know what you're talking about," she murmured. "I don't see what all this has to do with molting."

"Some of those signs," Aunt Polly explained, "mean an early winter; and some of 'em mean a cold one. I've never known 'em to fail. And you're molting early so you'll have a good warm coat of feathers by the time winter comes."

Well, Henrietta Hen began to feel better at once. She actually smiled— something she had not done for days.

"Thank you! Thank you!" she said. "You're a fine doctor, Aunt Polly. I don't wonder that folks ask your advice—especially when there's nothing the matter with them!"

And then Henrietta Hen hurried off down the lane. Being timid about hawks, she never felt quite comfortable far from the farmyard.

XX

A GREAT FLURRY

There was a great flurry among Farmer Green's hens. They all insisted on talking at the same time, because they had heard an astonishing bit of news. It was about Henrietta Hen. Wherever she went her neighbors craned their necks at her, just as if they hadn't seen her every day for as long as they could remember.

Henrietta Hen enjoyed the notice that everybody took of her. She went to some trouble to move about a good deal, so that all might have a chance to stare at her. For if there was one thing she liked, it was attention.

There was a reason why Henrietta had suddenly become the most talked-of member of the flock. She was going to the county fair! Furthermore, she expected to take all her children with her. There wasn't the least doubt that it was all true. The whole flock had heard Johnnie Green and his father talking about it.

Of course everybody asked Henrietta Hen a great number of questions. When was she going to leave? How long did she expect to stay at the fair? What did she intend to do there? Would she wear her best clothes if it rained? There was no end to such inquiries.

Unfortunately, Henrietta Hen could answer very few of them. Never having visited a fair, she had no idea what a fair was like. She only guessed that when the time came, she and her family would be put into a pen, loaded upon a wagon, and jolted over the road that led to the fair, wherever it might be.

But Henrietta didn't intend to let her neighbors find out how little she knew about fairs. She said that before starting she expected to wait for the wagon, that she hoped to stay at the fair as long as it lasted (because she didn't want to miss anything!) and that she intended to come home when the wagon brought her. Furthermore, she planned to wear her best apron, anyhow, because there was sure to be fair weather at a fair! How could it be otherwise?

Old Ebenezer, the horse, told her to be sure to see the races.

"They're the best part of a fair," he said. "In my younger days I used to take part in them." And then he added, "There's nothing else at a fair that's worth looking at."

"What about the poultry show?" Henrietta Hen asked him. She didn't know what poultry shows were; but she had heard Farmer Green mention them.

"I never paid any attention to the poultry exhibit," the horse Ebenezer replied. "I never took part in that. I suppose it might interest you, however."

Henrietta Hen smiled a knowing sort of smile. And she remarked to Polly Plymouth Rock, who stood near her, that she didn't believe the old horse knew a race from a poultry show. "If he ever went to a fair, I dare say he was hitched outside the fence," she sniffed.

Polly Plymouth Rock cackled with amusement. And she said something that displeased Henrietta Hen exceedingly.

"Are you going to take that duckling that you hatched out?" she asked.

"Certainly not!" Henrietta snapped. "Please—Miss Plymouth Rock—never mention him again! I'm going to the fair, among strangers. And I shouldn't care to have them know about that accident that happened to me—not for anything!"

XXI

OFF FOR THE FAIR

It seemed to Henrietta Hen that the time for the fair would never come. She had begun to feel somewhat uneasy, because she had talked so much about visiting the fair with her children that it would be very awkward if she didn't go. So she was delighted one day by the noise of hammering and sawing that came from the workbench at the end of the wagon-shed. A merry noise it was, to Henrietta's ears; for she guessed at once what was happening. Farmer Green and his son were building a pen in which she and her family were to ride to the fair!

The news spread like fire in sun-dried grass. Henrietta Hen took pains that it should. She told everybody she saw that she expected to leave at any moment. And she began to say good-by to all her friends.

Since Henrietta didn't start for the fair that day, before nightfall she had bade every one farewell at least a dozen times. And when, the following dawn, Henrietta started the day not by saying "Good morning!" but by bidding her neighbors "Good-by!" once more, they began to think her a bit tiresome.

"What! Haven't you gone yet?" they asked her.

"No! But I expect to leave at any moment," Henrietta told them. She was so excited that she couldn't eat her breakfast. But her chicks had no such trouble. And perhaps it was just as well that Henrietta Hen had her hands full looking after them and trying to keep them all under her eye, and spick-and-span for the journey. Otherwise she would have been in more of a flutter than she was.

While Henrietta had an eye on her children, she tried to keep the other on the barn. And after what seemed to her hours of watching and waiting, she saw Johnnie Green lead the old horse Ebenezer out of the door, with his harness on. Henrietta promptly forgot her stately manners. She ran squalling across the farmyard and called to Ebenezer, "Where are you going?"

"I understand that I'm going to the fair," he told her, as Johnnie Green backed him between the thills of a wagon. "Once I would have been hitched to a light buggy, with a sulky tied behind it. But now I've got to take you and your family in this rattlety old contraption."

Henrietta Hen didn't wait to hear any more. She turned and hurried back, to gather her youngsters and bid everybody another farewell.

Amid a great clucking and squawking, Johnnie Green and his father put Henrietta and her chicks into the pen and placed it in the back of the wagon.

"We're all ready!" Henrietta cried to Ebenezer. The old horse didn't even turn his head, for he could see backwards as well as forwards, because he wore no blinders. He made no direct reply to Henrietta, though he gave a sort of grunt, as if the whole affair did not please him. He knew that it was a long distance to the fairgrounds and the road was hilly.

"She thinks it a lark," he said to the dog Spot, who hung about as if he were waiting for something. "She's lucky, for she won't have to go on her own legs, for miles and miles."

"That's just what I intend to do," Spot informed him. "They don't mean to take me. But I'm going to follow you, right under the wagon, where Johnnie Green and his father can't see me."

So they started off. And they had scarcely passed through the gate when Henrietta began to clamor in her shrillest tones. But nobody paid any heed to her. The wagon clattered off down the road. And old dog Spot smiled to himself as he trotted along beneath it.

"Henrietta just remembered that she forgot to put on her best apron," he chuckled.

XXII

ALMOST HOMESICK

Never in all her life had Henrietta Hen seen so many hens and roosters and chicks as she found on every side of her, at the fair. Farmer Green and his son Johnnie had set her pen in the Poultry Hall. And to Henrietta's surprise, none of her new neighbors paid much attention to her and her chicks—at first. She soon decided that there was a reason for this neglect. She made up her mind that she would have to make herself heard amid all that uproar or the others would never know she had arrived.

Luckily Henrietta had a strong voice. She used it to the utmost. And it wasn't long before a huge hen in a pen next hers gave her a bold look and asked, "What are you here for?"

"I've come to get the first prize," Henrietta answered calmly. She had listened carefully to what Farmer Green and Johnnie had said to each other during the journey from the farm. And already she knew something about fairs.

Her new neighbor laughed right in Henrietta's face.

"I don't see how you can win the first prize," she said with a sniff. "I'm going to get the first prize myself. There never was another such fine family as mine." She glanced proudly at her chicks as she spoke. "The best you can hope for," she told Henrietta, "is the second prize. And you'll be lucky if you get the third."

For once Henrietta Hen was at a loss for a retort.

"I don't believe you've ever been at a fair before," her new neighbor observed.

Henrietta admitted faintly that she hadn't.

"Last year I won second prize," said the other. "I'd have had the first if the judges had known their business."

Henrietta Hen began to feel very shaky in her legs. She had expected a different sort of greeting, when she should arrive at the fair. She had

48

thought everybody would exclaim, "Here comes Henrietta Hen! What a fine family of chicks she has! And aren't Mrs. Hen's speckles beautiful?"

And there she was, with nobody paying any heed to her, except the lofty dame in the next pen, who had said nothing very agreeable.

"Oh, dear!" Henrietta sighed. "I wish I'd never left home."

"What's that?" her neighbor inquired in a sharp tone. "You aren't homesick, are you?"

"N-no!" said Henrietta. "But I had expected to win the first prize. And I don't know what my friends will say when I come back home without it."

"Well, everybody can't win it," said her new acquaintance. "Not the same year, anyhow!" And then she looked Henrietta up and down for a few moments, while Henrietta squirmed uneasily. "Where do you come from?" she asked at last.

"I live on Farmer Green's place, in Pleasant Valley," Henrietta informed her.

The lady in the next pen shook her head. "I've never heard of Pleasant Valley," she remarked, "nor of Farmer Green. He must be small potatoes."

Well, Henrietta was astonished. She began to feel as if she were nobody at all. She had supposed that everybody knew of Pleasant Valley—and of Farmer Green, too. As for the remark, "small potatoes," she didn't understand it at all. So she inquired what it meant.

"It means," said her neighbor, "that Farmer Green can't be of much account."

That speech made Henrietta Hen almost lose her temper.

"Mr. Green," she cried, "is a fine man. And I'll have you know that I wouldn't live anywhere but on his farm!"

GETTING ACQUAINTED

Not liking her neighbor on her right, at the fair, Henrietta Hen sidled up to the wire netting on the opposite side of her pen. Peering through it, she examined the person whom she saw just beyond, in a pen of her own.

A very sleek hen was this, who gave Henrietta a slight nod.

"We may as well speak," she said, "since we're to live next to each other for a week."

"A week!" Henrietta groaned. "Shall I have to stay cooped up here as long as that?"

"Yes!" said Neighbor Number 2. "And I don't blame you for feeling as you seem to. A week is a long time for everybody here—except me."

Henrietta Hen didn't understand her.

"I'm going to win the first prize—with my chicks," Neighbor Number 2 announced. "Of course that's worth waiting here a week."

"I don't see how you can win the first prize!" Henrietta exclaimed.

"Why not?" demanded the other. And she pressed against the wire netting of her pen and stuck her head through it as far as she could, as if she would have pecked Henrietta had she been able to.

"Because—" Henrietta explained—"because the lady on the other side of me is going to win it."

"Who said so?"

"She did," Henrietta answered.

"Ha! ha!" cackled Neighbor Number 2. "That's a good joke. She hasn't any more chance of winning than—than you have!"

Now, Henrietta Hen couldn't help being puzzled. But whoever might win the first prize, she was sure it couldn't be she. Hadn't her neighbors on either side of her the same as told her that she couldn't win?

Henrietta would have felt quite glum, except that she couldn't very well mope in the midst of the terrific racket all about her. Soon her neighbors — both Number 1 and Number 2 — were having loud disputes with the hens in the pens on the further side of them. It seemed as if every hen at the fair had left her manners at home — if she ever had any.

"Goodness!" Henrietta Hen murmured to herself. "If there's a prize, it must be for the one that can make the most noise."

In a little while throngs of men, women and children crowded into the Poultry Hall. They paused before the pens and looked at the occupants, making remarks that were sometimes full of praise and sometimes slighting.

Henrietta Hen felt terribly uneasy when people began to stop and stare at her. She dreaded to hear what they would say. After the way her next-door neighbors had talked to her she didn't believe anybody would have a word of praise for her.

She soon heard all sorts of remarks about herself. Some said she was too little and some said she was too big; others exclaimed that her legs were too short, while still others declared that they were too long! As these — and many similar — comments fell upon Henrietta's ears she promptly decided that there wasn't anything about her that was as it should be.

Having always called herself (before she left home) a "speckled beauty," she began to feel very low in her mind. And there was only one thing that kept her from being downright sad. All the sightseers agreed that she had some pretty chicks.

Henrietta couldn't help wishing that they had a different mother — one that was worthy of them.

XXIV

WINNING FIRST PRIZE

Henrietta Hen was waiting as patiently as she could for the fair to come to an end. She tried to close her ears to the boasts of her neighbors on either side of her, that they were going to win the first prize. She had heard too many unpleasant remarks about herself to have even the slightest hope of winning any prize at all—let alone the first.

"Anyhow, we'll be going home tonight," Henrietta said to herself. "And I'll never, never, never come to another fair. I'll go and hide 'way up high in the haymow where they can't find me before I'll spend another week in a place like this."

While she was muttering under her breath like that some men came up to her pen. And Henrietta Hen promptly squatted down in the furthest corner of it, hoping they wouldn't say anything disagreeable about her. She felt that she had already heard about all she could stand. She didn't even look at her callers. And soon they moved away.

Then Henrietta glanced up. She noticed something blue dangling from the front of her pen. And there was a greater commotion than ever on all sides of her.

"What is it?" she cried. "What has happened?"

Neighbor Number 1, on her right, shot a spiteful look at her.

"Those stupid judges!" she spluttered. "They've made a terrible blunder. They've gone and given you and your chicks the first prize. And of course it was meant for me and mine!"

"It wasn't!" screamed Neighbor Number 2 (on Henrietta's left). "That prize was intended for me and my children!"

"Who won second and third?" cried a noisy hen from across the way.

"They're both at the other end of the hall!" somebody shrieked.

"It's an outrage! It isn't fair! We've been cheated!" Henrietta Hen's nearest neighbors clamored. But nobody paid any attention to them.

52

As for Henrietta, she didn't quite know how to act. She had intended, when she left home, to do a good deal of strutting back and forth in her pen, with now and then a pause to preen herself, to make sure that she looked her best. But somehow she no longer cared to put on grand airs, as of old. She remembered that some of the other hens at the fair had been haughty and proud and had smoothed their feathers, declaring boldly that they expected to win the first prize.

Henrietta had heard it said that fine feathers don't make fine birds. And she knew at last what that meant. It meant that gay clothes and lofty ways and boastful talk were of no account at all.

So Henrietta tried to behave as if nothing unusual had happened. She told her chicks that they were going home that evening, and that she would be glad to be back on the farm again, among plain home-folks.

At last Johnnie Green and his father came to load Henrietta and her family into the wagon.

"Well," said the old horse Ebenezer to Henrietta. "Did you enjoy the races?"

"I didn't have a chance to see them," she replied.

"That's a pity," he told her. And then he asked her, "What's that blue tag hanging from your pen?"

"That—" said Henrietta—"that means that my chicks won the first prize."

"She helped win it herself," cried old dog Spot, who was yelping about the wagon. "Our little speckled hen was the best hen at the fair!"

"Nonsense!" Henrietta exclaimed. But, all the same, she couldn't help being pleased.

THE END